MW01031088

Loving Luke

BY CECELIA DOWDY

When Kim Taylor returns to Bethlehem to run her family's cookie shop, her life is in shambles. She doesn't get along with her dad, and she secretly longs to fix their broken relationship.

She's stunned when Luke Barnes, her former high school boyfriend, strolls into her cookie shop. Recently widowed, Luke has returned to Bethlehem to raise his daughter, Lisa, in a wholesome environment.

Seeing Kim reawakens Luke's memories from long ago. Their high-school romance is a painful reminder of the man he used to be. However, falling for Kim is not on his agenda right now. Luke is struggling with a problem, and it looks like Kim is the only person that can help him solve his dilemma.

Luke has already hurt her once, so, can she find the courage to trust him again?

LOVING LUKE
Copyright © 2015 Cecelia Dowdy

LOVING LUKE is published by Divine Desserts Publishing.

All rights reserved. No part of this book may be used or reproduced in any form or by any electronic or mechanical means, including information storage and retrieval systems, without written permission from the author.

This book is a work of fiction. Any reference to historical or contemporary figures, places, or events, whether fictional or actual, is a fictional representation. Any resemblance to actual persons living or dead is entirely coincidental.

All rights reserved. No part of this book may be used or reproduced in any manner whatsoever without written permission from the author except in the case of brief quotations embodied in critical articles or reviews.

Cover Design by Elizabeth Mackey at Elizabeth Mackey Designs.

Interior Format

Loving Luke

CHAPTER 1

THE CHUGGING ECHO OF A motorcycle rolled down Main Street. Kim grabbed her oven mitts, the loud sound bringing memories of her wild high school days in Bethlehem. The noise stopped just as she pulled the hot tray of vanilla cookies from the oven. The heated warmth surrounded her face as she sniffed the sweet scent. Sweat beaded her brow, and she placed the tray onto a rack before wiping her forehead with a clean towel.

She removed the box of edible silver sprinkles from the shelf just as the Christmas sleigh bells above the front door jingled. She glanced toward the entrance, spotting Luke Barnes strolling into her cookie shop! Startled, her heart skipped a beat and she dropped the box of sprinkles. Tiny silver balls rolled on the floor, and she inwardly groaned, picking up the box and shoving it onto the table.

"Luke." She couldn't even think of what she should say. "I didn't realize you were back in Bethlehem." She walked toward the counter, the silver-ball sprinkles crunching beneath her shoes.

She resisted the urge to come from behind the counter to hug him. His dark eyes seemed a bit wary, almost as if he'd been unsure about entering her cookie shop.

She had not seen Luke since her junior year in high school, so, why should his sudden presence make her act like a love-sick teenager? She shouldn't let his presence rattle her.

But it did.

He finally nodded toward her. "Kim, it's been awhile."

"It sure has." Eight years to be exact. It was surprising what eight years could do to a person. He still had an enticing, mocha-colored complexion, but, he now sported a full mustache and beard. He looked…bigger, as if he'd grown or gained weight since high school.

She swallowed and took a deep breath. They'd gotten matching dove tattoos when they were dating. She eyed her hand, still sporting the scar that was the result of her having her tattoo surgically removed.

He glanced toward the floor, scratching the back of his neck. "I didn't realize you were in town either until last night."

"Oh?" Had he stopped by just to see her, hoping to rekindle old memories?

He studied the cookie shop. "This place hasn't changed much."

She'd put up the Christmas decorations that morning, placing red poinsettias on the four small tables in the front. White temporary paint frosted the large windows, giving the effect of a snowy Christmas day.

Luke glanced at the cookie display, as if he were deciding what he wanted to buy. Her dad had taken the afternoon off to go to a dentist appointment, and, for some reason, Kim was glad that her father wasn't here right now. Seeing Luke rattled her, and she could imagine her dad questioning her after Luke's unexpected visit.

He continued studying the cookies. "I've only been back since August. It's surprising to see you working in your parents' bakery."

Kim stood at the counter, waiting. She didn't feel like correcting Luke, telling him that only her dad owned the bakery now that her mom was deceased or that she'd been to college and until recently, had worked as an accountant in Chicago. She pushed the thoughts from her mind, again focusing on Luke. For some reason, she doubted he wanted to hear about her life since he'd disappeared from Bethlehem.

Luke shoved his hands into the pockets of his pants, jiggling his keys and change. She recalled he usually did this when he was nervous. She cleared her throat, glanced at the clock. Her dad would be back soon, and before he returned, she wanted to figure out what Luke wanted. "Did you come to buy cookies?"

"I…" he paused, glanced at the display. "I'll take a dozen chocolate chip."

She grinned. Memories of eating warm chocolate chip cookies and cold glasses of milk with Luke Barnes unfurled in her mind like snowflakes dancing in the wind. Despite her parents' objections, she'd baked batches of Luke's favorite chocolate chip cookies and would secretly meet him at his house. After sharing hot cookies, they'd drink cold milk from the same glass. Luke would always kiss her, telling her how much he loved her and her cookies. Their kisses had always turned passionate, and she shook the thought away, not wanting to dwell on what usually happened after those kisses. Her life was a lot different now that she was saved, but, she still had some regrets over her past mistakes.

She glanced up, caught Luke staring at her with his mesmerizing dark brown eyes. Had he been thinking of the times they'd shared, eating cookies and milk? No way was she going to ask him about that. She boxed up the cookies, rang up the order. After he'd paid, he still stood at the register, hesitating, holding the pastel, monogrammed bakery box. "Yes?" she prompted.

His hand was still shoved in his pocket and he fidgeted. "Look, I didn't come here to buy cookies."

"Oh?"

"My daughter told me she wanted to work here."

Kim frowned. What in the world was he talking about? Another thing she recalled about Luke, he was terrible at giving details. When he told her something, she'd always felt like she was only getting half of the story and she'd have to ask questions, forcing him to fill in the blanks. "You have a daughter?" Was he referring to the child he'd fathered in high school?

He nodded. "Yes, I'm talking about Lisa. You met her at school, right?"

"My goodness. The little girl from Career Day is your daughter?" She never would've guessed that

Lisa was Luke's daughter. So mind-boggling that Luke, a man from her past, was now in her bakery because his nine-year-old daughter wanted to make cookies with her after school.

The previous day, Kim had participated in the annual Career Day at Bethlehem Elementary School. Career Day always took place the Monday after the Thanksgiving holiday. When Kim had asked for a volunteer to help with her staged demonstration, she'd ended up picking a cute, shy-looking child named Lisa. Since part of the Career Day activities included job mentorship, she'd offered to have Lisa come visit the cookie shop and help her bake cookies.

"She'd said you'd offered her a job."

"Not exactly a job. I'd just invited her over for an after-school cookie baking session." No way was she telling him about Lisa's complaints regarding his burning cookies and his failed attempts at making dinner. "We're usually busy during the Christmas season and if she wants to come and help after school for a day, she can." She paused. "I don't know if she'd want to come regularly to help bake cookies. I thought we'd try it for a day or so, and see what happens from there, if that's okay with you."

He shook his head. "I don't know if it's okay for Lisa to be here with you."

She stepped away from the counter, silently counting to ten, gritting her teeth. "What do you mean by that?"

"Come on, Kim. You know what I mean. You were so wild in high school."

"So were you," she countered, balling her hands

into fists, trying to control her temper. He had a lot of nerve, riding here on his motorcycle, implying she'd be a bad influence on his daughter.

He set the cookie box on a nearby table, held his hands up. "Hey, don't get mad. I'm just saying I've got to be careful where my daughter is concerned."

"You're basing your opinion of me on the way I was eight years ago and that's not fair. I'm not the same person as I was back then." A thought occurred to her. "Are you the same as you were eight years ago or have you changed?"

"I'm a Christian now and –"

"So am I." She'd accepted Christ a year after Luke had abandoned her. The kids at Bethlehem High School had gossiped about Luke's desertion for months afterwards. She'd even asked some of his friends if they had a way to contact him, but, they couldn't help her locate Luke. She couldn't find anything about him on social media. It was almost as if Luke didn't want to be found once he left Bethlehem.

He furrowed his brow, as if he didn't believe her. "You're really a Christian?"

She nodded. Why was this so hard to believe? Eight years was a long time and a lot of stuff could happen. Luke claimed he'd been in town since August, yet, she had not seen him or Lisa at Bethlehem Community Church. It was possible that they worshipped elsewhere, though.

He glanced uneasily at her, scratching the back of his neck. Kim decided she'd felt rattled enough for one day. She didn't want her father returning and asking questions about her strange reaction to Luke. Her dad could read her like a book, and he'd know she was unsettled. She needed some time to calm down before her father returned from the dentist. Besides, she needed to frost the vanilla cookies before her customer arrived to pick up the order. "Look, why don't you think about it and when you decide what you want to do, then call me."

Luke gave her a quick nod, lifting his cookie box from the table. The sleigh bells jingled as he exited the bakery.

As soon as Luke drove away, the sound of his motorcycle echoing in the bakery, Kim pulled her phone from her pocket, texting her best friends, Carly, Anna and Heather. The four of them had been best friends since elementary school. Since they'd been friends with her when she'd dated Luke, she figured they'd be interested in knowing that he was back in town. She began her text: *Ladies, Luke Barnes is back in Bethlehem.*

As soon as she'd sent the text, her phone buzzed. She eyed the display, seeing that her friend Heather was calling. "Heather, I can't believe Luke just came into my bakery. He really made me mad."

"What did he say?"

Kim put her phone onto the speaker setting, went back into the kitchen, telling Heather all about her conversation with Luke. She dropped softened butter and the rest of the frosting ingredients into a large bowl. After she was done speaking to Heather, she needed to frost the wedding-bell shaped cookies. Her customer would be arriving later to take the cookies to an office bridal shower.

"Hmm." Heather appeared to be in deep thought. "Seems like a strange coincidence that Luke, your high school ex-boyfriend would come to your shop, right when you're struggling to get over your ex-fiancé."

Kim groaned, glancing at the cookies. Just looking at the wedding-bell shaped treats caused vivid memories of her aborted wedding plans, nearly one year ago, to unfurl in her mind. "What's your point?"

"Maybe the Lord wants you and Luke to rekindle your high school romance."

Kim pressed her lips together. That was the dumbest thing she'd ever heard. Luke didn't even want his daughter to spend time with her. Rekindling their romance was probably the furthest thing from his mind.

She hadn't been saved when she'd dated him in high school and they'd had a torrid relationship. They'd both been young and immature, and she'd recalled how hurt she'd been when he'd gotten Salina Foster pregnant. After he'd abruptly left town with his mom and Salina, not even bothering to say good-bye to her, she'd been devastated. She had not been able to get over her pain until she'd left home and started college.

"I think you're wrong." After the shock of seeing Luke and disagreeing with him, she felt she needed something to calm herself down. A cookie, yes, that's what she needed. She needed a cookie fix to make herself feel better.

"Well, I think I'm right. There must be some

kind of chemistry between the two of you if you're mad at him after one short conversation."

This conversation with Heather was not making her feel better. "I have to go." She ended the call, lifted a warm cookie from the rack, her stomach growling with hunger. Biting into the treat, the sweet taste of vanilla and sugar exploded on her tongue and she sighed, leaning back against the wall. Eating this cookie lifted her mood, just a little bit.

These were the best vanilla cookies she'd ever tasted in her entire life, and her heart swelled, recalling how long it had taken her and her deceased mom to develop the recipe, years ago. Unable to resist, she gobbled another cookie, continuing to think about Luke. He'd looked as good as he did back in high school, if not better. It had just seemed weird to see Luke riding a motorcycle while wearing slacks and loafers. Back in high school, he'd worn ripped jeans, a t-shirt and a leather jacket when riding his motorbike.

Continuing to feast on dessert, she closed her eyes, thinking about the last three months of her life. Returning to Bethlehem a few months ago to work in her family's bakery had been bittersweet. It'd been eight years since she'd left Bethlehem. She'd hoped that the work of baking cookies in the hot kitchen, spending time with her dad, would help her to heal from the pain of her ex-fiancé's infidelity, and help her deal with her mom's recent death. It'd been eleven months since that fateful day of her breakup, and whenever she thought about her ex, her heart pounded and tears rushed to her eyes. Being in love was like a toxic disease and she didn't know when she'd have the courage to fall in love again. Why couldn't God lift away this awful pain? How long would it take for her to heal?

CHAPTER 2

SITTING IN HIS CAR, LUKE stared at his smart phone, wincing. His professor had posted their grades online that morning. He'd gotten a *D* on his calculus quiz and he didn't know what he was going to do to pull his grade up.

"What are you looking at, Dad?" Lisa peeked over his shoulder from the back seat. He darkened the screen, throwing the phone on the passenger seat. No way did he want his nine-year-old daughter to see he'd gotten a bad grade on his quiz. He'd always taught Lisa the importance of doing well in school. The last thing he needed was for her to see that he was setting a bad example.

"Did you pack your lunch?" He ignored her question, wanting her to focus on something else.

She rolled her eyes, opening her car door. "Of course I packed my lunch. I did my homework and I have my books in my backpack." She looked at him, narrowing her dark eyes, eyes that looked so much like her mom's that it tugged at his heart. "Why did you park in the school parking lot? You usually just drop me off in front of the school." She fingered her long dark hair, which was pulled back into a ponytail. Since they'd moved to Bethlehem, she'd gotten more concerned about the way she looked. He still couldn't believe the time and expense it had taken for her to get her hair done the previous week.

Again, he ignored her question, unsure of how to give a diplomatic response. How did you tell a nine-year-old child that you were trying to investigate the reputation of your former high-school girlfriend? "I'm coming into the school with you."

Lisa's mouth dropped open as she slid the backpack onto her back. "Dad, that's so lame. Only little kids have their parents walk into the school with them." She took a few steps away from him, as if being in his presence would ruin her reputation. "You're treating me like I'm in kindergarten and I don't like it."

"Don't use that tone with me." He glared at Lisa until she relaxed her shoulders and they made their way into the school together.

The previous night, Lisa had mentioned that Kim was a volunteer math tutor at the school. When he'd gone to bed, he had dreamed about his visit to Kim's cookie shop. Seeing her had been like viewing a ray of sunshine on a dark cloudy day. She was just as pretty as she'd been in high school. Her smooth chocolate brown skin, full lips, and deep soulful eyes enticed him, made him question all that they'd been through. The what-ifs now plagued his mind. What if he'd never left Bethlehem, would they have found a way to make their relationship work, in spite of his infidelity?

He'd offended Kim by insinuating that she'd be

a bad influence on his daughter. He'd gotten out of bed, and curious, he'd Googled Kim Taylor and found that she was listed on the Bethlehem Elementary School's website as a volunteer. Seeing her name posted there had given him a bit of reassurance about her reputation. He figured he'd ask Lisa's teacher if she knew Kim.

He'd also discovered that Kim's mom had died shortly before he'd moved back to Bethlehem. Shocked, he'd found an entire article about her mother in the newspaper, along with the obituary. He'd recalled Kim's mother had been a sweet lady, and he'd closed his eyes, thinking about the time he'd known Kim's mom while he'd been in high school.

Lord, please help Kim and her dad. The pain of unexpectedly losing his wife still sliced through him, even though she'd been dead for over a year. He figured Kim and her father were suffering right now. He pushed the tragic thoughts from his mind, studying his daughter as they made their way into the school. She continued to walk quickly, placing as much distance between them as possible. Several kids rushed down the hallway, trying to make it to their class before the bell rang. Colorful artwork and class calendars partially covered the white tiled walls. The bell rang just as Lisa and Luke entered the classroom. Lisa ignored him, rushing to her desk.

Lisa's teacher approached. "Mr. Barnes, hello." The young woman greeted him, shaking his hand.

Luke nodded, releasing her hand. "Ms. Cummings."

She batted her lashes and he tried not to laugh.

During back-to-school night, Lisa's teacher had made a point to spend as much time talking to him afterwards as possible. When he'd first arrived in Bethlehem, the last thing on his mind was dating anybody, especially Lisa's teacher.

He gestured toward the door. "Do you mind if I talk to you for a minute?"

The young woman's light brown skin flushed, and he had to wonder if she were blushing. She stepped into the hallway, closing the classroom door behind her. "I'm so glad you asked to speak with me. I figured you'd lost my number."

He shook his head, baffled. "I'm sorry?"

"Remember, I gave you my phone number on back-to-school night. I'd offered to show you around, help you get more acquainted with Bethlehem."

That was an experience he'd chosen to forget. Good thing Lisa had no problems in school and had exceled in all of her subjects. If he went to Ms. Cummings for any kind of help, she'd probably take his intentions the wrong way. "I came to ask you about Kim."

The woman's eyes widened as she stared at the dove tattoo decorating his hand. "Kim? Who is Kim?"

He shoved his hand into his pocket. The tattoo was just another reminder of his former days in Bethlehem, as well as his torrid relationship with Kim. After getting drunk one night, they'd gone out of town and gotten tattoos. Afterwards, Kim had been grounded for two months, and at that time, it'd been the worse two months of his life. "Kim Taylor."

"Why on earth would you be asking me about Kim Taylor?" The teacher now seemed impatient as she glanced at her watch, tapping her foot. He was doing a terrible job of explaining.

"Kim offered Lisa a job working in her bakery. I wasn't sure if it was a good idea for Lisa to work with Kim."

The woman's face softened into a smile. "Oh, Kim's the best. She tutors students in math and all of the kids and the staff like her. I think Lisa could learn a lot from her. The school office does background checks on all of their volunteers, so, you don't have anything to worry about."

That was a relief. He nodded at her. "Thanks."

"Was there anything else?" Her large, dark brown eyes looked hopeful as she again batted her lashes.

"No, that's it." He needed to get out of there. If he lingered much longer, he'd be late for work.

Later, Luke strolled through the sliding glass doors of the marketing firm, exiting the building, holding his cell phone. It was time for lunch, but, he wasn't hungry. His co-workers were commenting about his behavior that day, stating he'd not seemed focused on his work, and when they spoke to him, he'd not heard them and they'd had to repeat themselves.

He strolled to the sandwich shop across the street. What a night he'd had. After looking for information about Kim on the internet, he'd then thought about his class. The next calculus exam loomed in the distance, and he wasn't ready. He just didn't seem to have an aptitude for the higher level math subjects, but, he needed to take the business calculus course as a requirement for his Associate's degree. He'd studied until three in the morning, figuring he'd need to find a tutor.

He entered John's Sports Bar and Sandwich Shop, approached the counter.

"Hey, Luke." The server's white apron stretched across his bulging stomach. He wiped down the counter. "What'll you have?"

"Hey, John. Tuna on rye and a Coke."

John gestured toward the stools. "You sitting at the bar?"

No way did he want to sit at the bar today. From his experience, sitting at the bar meant you wanted to talk and he didn't want to encourage conversation with John, or any of the customers right now. He just wanted to be left alone. He scanned the crowded place, finding a small empty table in the corner. "Just bring my food over there." He gestured toward the spot before he approached the empty table. He then removed his coat before dropping into the chair.

The small sandwich shop bustled with activity as customers filtered into the glass doors. Waiting for his food, he glanced outside, still thinking about Kim. He'd noticed the wounded look in her pretty eyes when he'd told her that he didn't know if his daughter should spend time with her. He remembered that look so well. Kim always looked like that when she'd told him that her father loved her sister, Tina, more than he loved her. Usually, after they'd made love, she'd be open and honest with him about her feelings, not being the tough girl others thought she was. She'd told him how much it hurt her when she heard her father brag about Tina, his perfect daughter.

He knew she'd been mad when he'd hinted at his disapproval of her spending time with Lisa. But, his daughter was the most important person to him on this God-given earth, and he wanted to raise her in the best way possible. When he'd moved to Bethlehem, he'd even considered sending her to a private school, but, he simply could not afford it on his marketing clerk salary. The most important reason why he was going to school was so that he could make more money to provide a better life for his daughter.

John approached his table, leaving his sandwich and drink. "There ya go."

Luke nodded, said a prayer, before taking a bite of his tuna on rye. He knew he'd over-reacted and he didn't want to hurt Kim's feelings. He needed to call Kim and let her know that Lisa could come by after school tomorrow if it was okay with her. He also needed to explain why he seemed so over-protective of his daughter. He figured he'd tell Kim about that when he saw her again.

Finishing his sandwich, he removed his cell phone from his pocket and dialed the phone number for Kim's bakery.

CHAPTER 3

KIM SLICED THE FUDGE BROWNIES into neat squares, her stomach growling. She hadn't had lunch yet and she resisted the urge to shove a few of these into her mouth. The rich chocolate scent filled the kitchen. Sniffing, she relished the delicious aroma. The phone rang and she put her knife aside. Her father was occupied with customers in the front of the bakery. "Taylor's Cookie Shop."

"Kim." Her heart skipped. It was Luke. His distinctive deep voice was easy to recognize. "This is Luke."

"Yes?" He was probably calling to tell her that he didn't want his daughter working in her cookie bakery. She probably didn't measure up to his standards. But, he was entitled to his opinion. She wouldn't let his rejection bother her, after all, he was only thinking about his daughter's well-being.

"Lisa can help you in the bakery, if you want her to."

This was a surprise. "Really?"

"Yes."

"She can come today if you want."

He hesitated. "Are you sure?"

"Yes."

"Well, I hadn't planned on letting her come today. I wasn't sure how she was going to get from the school to the bakery."

The school was within walking distance to the bakery, and Kim understood Luke hesitating about letting his daughter walk the few blocks alone. "My dad is here to watch the bakery. So, I can go pick her up after school."

"Okay. I'll let her teacher know that you'll be picking her up."

"Good." They agreed on a pickup time before he ended the call.

Luke pushed the door open to her shop, causing the overhead sleigh bells to ring. Every time a customer had entered this evening, Kim had looked toward the door, anticipating Luke's arrival. She came from behind the counter, about to close up. It'd been a busy afternoon since they'd been getting a lot of requests for Christmas cookies.

Lisa grinned. "Dad, I had the best time!" She retrieved her backpack, holding a box of cookies in her hand. "We made vanilla cookies. Did you know that vanilla comes from a bean? You scrape the seeds out of this dark black bean and use them in the cookies. Dad, they are so good!"

The excitement in Lisa's voice made Kim's heart skip. Lisa's enthusiastic attitude had really helped brightened her afternoon.

As Lisa chattered to her dad, Kim stared at Luke. He looked…good. So handsome. Memories of their high-school romance filled her mind, and she took a deep breath, pushing the thoughts away. Her relationship with Luke had happened a long time ago, and she couldn't let herself fantasize about their previous mutual attraction. After all, that was ancient history. Last night, her friends Carly and Anna had texted her back, shocked that Luke was back in Bethlehem. They'd asked for more details but Kim could only confirm that Luke's daughter was working in her cookie shop, and that he'd initially made her mad. There wasn't much more that she could say.

Lisa continued chattering and Kim noticed the battered black backpack that Luke carried. The backpack had the emblem of Bethlehem Community College. She wondered if Luke was in school, but, didn't want to interrupt Lisa's chatter to ask. "Calm down, Lisa. You can tell me about everything when we get home."

"Can I come back tomorrow?"

Luke finally looked at her. She tried not to let those nice, dark brown eyes affect her. She hoped he said yes – it would give her an excuse to see him tomorrow. "You can come if Kim says it's okay."

Lisa looked at Kim. "Can I come back tomorrow? Please?" Lisa's voice took on a pleading tone, and Kim chuckled.

"Of course you can come back tomorrow."

Kim then studied Luke's face, noticing the dark circles under his eyes. He looked so tired, and she wanted to ask if he were having trouble sleeping, but, didn't want to be too nosy.

He glanced at his car, which was parked right outside the bakery. He removed his key fob and unlocked the car door. "Lisa, go wait for me in the car."

"Dad, I'm not too young to hear what you have to say to Ms. Kim."

"Do not argue with me. Go wait in the car." His deep, stark tone filled the room, and Lisa seemed to know that she needed to obey her dad. Huffing, Lisa finally exited the bakery, walked to the car and got inside. Luke re-locked the car door with his key fob before focusing on her.

Good gracious, he looked just as handsome as he did when they were in high school. Her breath caught. She just needed to stop staring at him and find out why he'd just sent his daughter out to the car. For the life of her, she couldn't imagine why he'd need to speak with her alone. "Mind if we sit for a few minutes?"

So, he wanted her to sit down? Just to talk? This was surprising. They settled into their chairs. "You look upset. Are you okay?"

He cleared his throat, looked toward the wall, before focusing on her again. "No, I feel bad. I know I offended you yesterday, implying that you'd be a bad influence on Lisa." Truth be told, she had been offended, but figured she couldn't let his opinion bother her too much. After all, she had enough on her mind already without having to worry about deciphering why Luke wouldn't want her around his daughter. "I just wanted to say that I'm sorry."

She nodded. "You don't have to apologize."

"Yes, I do. I owe you an explanation. My wife Salina was killed in a car accident a year and a half ago and my life hasn't been the same."

"Luke, I'm so sorry."

He fidgeted, just as he'd always done when he was anxious or upset. Just like during their high school days, she briefly touched his hand. When they'd dated, a simple touch could calm him down. He finally looked at her again. "I worry about Lisa, especially since Salina died. Initially, after Salina's death, I didn't want to let Lisa out of my sight. I'm slowly learning that raising Lisa is a day-to-day process, but, I find myself questioning all of my decisions, wanting to do what's best for her."

"Well, she's your daughter." She'd assume most parents felt this way about their children.

"I know but, I've been accused of going over-board, being over-protective of her."

"I accept your apology. Don't worry about it."

He relaxed, glanced at his battered backpack on the floor. She grinned, determined to put him at ease. "Why'd you bring your backpack into the shop?"

Returning her smile, he lifted the backpack off of the floor. "I've had a lot on my mind lately. I just brought the backpack out of habit. I usually take it with me to work and to the classes I have in the evenings." He stood up, going toward the door. "Thanks. I'll see you tomorrow then."

The corner of his backpack caught onto the door handle, and it ripped, causing his school books to spill from the backpack and onto the floor. Kim spotted his calculus book as he gathered his scattered pens and pencils. "You're taking calculus?"

Luke had barely passed Algebra in high school. Kim had helped him with his Algebra homework, and they'd sat beside one another in class and she'd let him cheat off her Algebra exams. Algebra had been the last subject they had in high school together before he'd moved away.

"Yes, it's awful. I'm up late, studying every night. I doubt I'll pass."

"Have you considered hiring a tutor?"

"Yes. I was going to talk to my professor about that after class tomorrow."

She didn't know if he'd agree to this idea, but, she might as well ask him. "Well, I don't mind helping."

"But this is calculus, not high school algebra."

Kim shrugged, secretly pleased that he remembered her helping him with Algebra in high school. "I took this class when I was getting my bachelor's." She removed the book from his hands, flipping through the pages. "I used this same text book."

"You have a bachelor's degree?" His shocked tone made her pause, until she recalled that he literally knew nothing about her life since he'd skipped town eight years ago. The only thing he knew was that she was a Christian now, and that she was currently running her family's cookie bakery. Heck, Luke probably thought that she'd never left Bethlehem after high school.

"Yes, I have a bachelor's degree. So, do you want my help or not?" She certainly wasn't going to beg him to accept her help, but, if he wasn't doing well in the class, he'd be foolish to turn down her offer.

His dark eyes widened as he took the book away

from her. "Yes, I want your help…"

"But?" Maybe he felt leery since they used to date in high school. Maybe he mistakenly felt that she might want to re-kindle their relationship while they worked on calculus equations.

"Look, I really want your help. I just feel guilty accepting your offer."

Kim frowned. "Why would you feel guilty?"

He took a deep breath, as if he were gathering his thoughts. "Well, Lisa sounds like she really likes coming here. I think she'll want to come here every day after school if she's allowed."

"I don't mind. She's a big help to me."

"But, you're already helping me with Lisa, and now accepting your help with my calculus class." He glanced at his car before focusing on her again. "Am I taking advantage of your time?"

"Well, I offered. If it turns out to be too much for me, I'll let you know." She didn't have much to occupy her time outside of the cookie bakery. "So, if you want my help, we need to decide when it'll be best for us to meet."

"As soon as possible. I'm failing."

"Seriously?"

He nodded. "I just don't understand this stuff, even if I stay up half the night studying."

It sounded like Luke needed some serious help. Kim honestly didn't know if she'd be able to prevent him from failing, but, she was certainly going to try. "How about I come over to your place on Saturday night? We could eat dinner before we start studying."

"Are you sure you want to eat my cooking?" He teased.

"How about I bring dinner with me?" She recalled Lisa telling her about Luke's aversion to cooking. In high school, Luke had loved the spicy chili she used to make. Since she'd re-located back to Bethlehem, she had not made any big meals. Her dad didn't have a big appetite and with just the two of them, she didn't have to cook very often. Her father often ate dinner at John's Sandwich Shop since a group of senior citizens congregated there during the evenings.

"Well..." he hesitated again. She touched his shoulder, wanting to put him at ease.

"It's okay. I don't mind cooking. My dad eats out a lot and I usually end up eating by myself." She inwardly winced. Her comment sounded so pathetic. Luke was probably thinking that she was a lonely single woman with too much time on her hands.

Luke finally nodded, accepting her offer. He squeezed her hand, gave her a quick hug and a kiss on the cheek, before rushing out to his car.

CHAPTER 4

KIM'S FATHER ENTERED THE KITCHEN, humming. He was dressed in jeans and a plaid shirt, his balding brown head shining under the bright kitchen lights. From his good mood, she suspected he'd recently spoken to her sister, Tina.

"Tina called earlier, when you went out for your lunch break." He lifted the lid of the crock pot, taking a large sniff. "That chili smells good."

"Thanks." The aroma of tomatoes, spices, and baking bread filled the air, making her mouth water. Kim pulled the hot pan of cornbread out of the oven. A nice bowl of chili and a slice of corn-bread slathered with butter sounded good on this cold, wintry evening. After placing the pan on the stove, she peeked out the kitchen window. Clouds were moving in. It looked like snow was coming. "What did Tina say?"

"She said she hadn't talked to you in a while. You should call your sister. She's been worried about you."

Kim resisted the urge to roll her eyes. She highly doubted Tina was worried about her. She was probably so busy with her perfect kids and perfect doctor husband that she barely had time to fret about others. Besides, Tina could easily call her if she really wanted to talk. "Dad, can I ask you something?"

"Sure."

"Why is it you're in such a good mood whenever Tina calls? I'm here every day, and my being here doesn't seem to lift your spirits."

"You always did get sassy over nothing. I just don't talk to Tina much, and it's good to hear from her. You're making a big deal out of nothing." He gestured toward the chili and cornbread. "You sure made a lot of food. I was going to meet my buddies over at the sandwich shop tonight." Kim figured they'd be sitting around, playing checkers and chess, talking about sports and current events.

"I was taking the food over to Luke's."

Her dad frowned, as if the thought of her making dinner for a man was a weird, foreign concept. "Luke who?"

"Luke Barnes."

"Luke Barnes? Are you nuts? Is this the guy you dated in high school who got that other girl pregnant? He made you miserable."

She pulled out the aluminum foil. The cornbread should still be warm when she got to Luke's if she covered it tightly. Lisa had only been helping in their bakery for a few days, and Kim's dad had not been in the bakery when Luke had come to fetch Lisa. She'd completely forgotten that her dad didn't know that Lisa's father was Luke Barnes. "Luke is Lisa's father."

"Oh, the cute kid who's been helping you in the

bakery?"

"Yes. They've only been in town for a few months." She went on to explain how she'd offered to help Luke with calculus and had offered to fix dinner, too.

"Humph. Well, looks like you're getting a little too comfortable with him, Little Girl, making dinner for him and all." She swallowed, stopping her food preparations. Her dad used to call her Little Girl when she was a kid, usually, he said this when he was worried or upset about something. "Look, I know you've been sad since your mom died. Spending time with Lisa might make you feel better, but, I don't want that boy to hurt you like he did the first time." He glanced at the crock pot before looking at her again, his mocha-colored face scrunched with worry. "You need to find yourself a nice, stable man. Find an educated man, someone who's like Anthony." Anthony was Tina's husband.

Kim gritted her teeth, resisting the urge to tell her father that she'd been engaged to a stable educated man who'd cheated on her. She'd mentioned Bill to her father, but, she'd never told her dad about her brief engagement to Bill. Since she'd moved back home, she'd wanted to tell her dad about her breakup, and about how she couldn't seem to get over how Bill had broken her trust. But, if she told him about that, he'd probably say that she'd been too naïve and trusting to see her boyfriend's faults. He patted her back before he left to go to the sandwich shop.

Her conversation with her father played through her mind as she loaded up the car and drove over to Luke's house. She knocked on his door and Lisa opened it. "Good, you're here! I'm hungry, and Dad told me that you were fixing dinner tonight!" Kim hugged Lisa, kissing her cheek. In just a few days' time, she'd grown fond of Luke's child.

Luke joined them in the living room. He looked wonderful. The exotic, manly scent of his after-shave was like a breath of fresh air. He wore a tee shirt and blue jeans. She caught herself staring at his brown, muscular arms. He hadn't been this muscular in high school, so, she imagined that he'd started working out sometime after he left Bethle-hem. With longing, she realized she wanted Luke to hug her again, but, he approached her, took her hand and squeezed it. His dark eyes full of sincerity. "Thanks for coming."

"You're welcome." She gestured toward his front door. "The food's in the car if you want to help me bring it in."

"Sure."

They went out into the frigid night and Luke carried the crock pot while Kim carried the corn-bread. Hopefully, he had the fixings for a salad. She'd meant to bring salad, too, but the conversa-tion with her dad had thrown her a bit off-kilter, made her forget. They feasted on cornbread, chili, and cucumber and tomato salad. After they were finished with dinner, Kim told Luke that he could keep the leftovers to eat tomorrow.

Luke made sure Lisa was occupied with her favorite movie and a bowl of popcorn in the liv-ing room while they settled down to study in the kitchen. As Kim had requested, Luke had made a list of all of the concepts he did not understand. They'd gotten one third of the way through the list, working out problems, while Kim attempted to explain the concept in a way that Luke would understand. Two hours later, Lisa announced she was tired. Luke sent her upstairs to get ready for bed.

He yawned. "I'm beat. We covered a lot in the last two hours."

She nodded, the conversation she'd had with her dad had hovered in the back of her mind while she'd been working with Luke. Truth be told, she was attracted to him, and deep down, she probably would be open to the idea of dating him again. She'd not been able to admit this to herself until her dad pointed it out to her. Was she being too forward, offering to help Luke, making dinner for him? Did Luke see her as some poor woman who was desperate for a man? She certainly hoped not.

He touched her face, and she jerked back, liking his gentle touch a little too much. "Hey, calm down. I'd just said something to you and you didn't respond. What's wrong?"

She shook her head. "Nothing's wrong, not really."

"Kim, you haven't changed a bit. As soon as you got here, I could see that something was bothering you. When you're upset, you don't always pay attention to what people are saying, almost like you're in a world of your own."

"Just something my dad said before I came here. Made me a little upset."

"Did it have anything to do with your sister, Tina?"

She glanced at him, surprised he'd remembered how much she disliked that her sister was the favored sibling in the Taylor household. "He did mention Tina." But, she just couldn't tell him what her dad said about her getting too comfortable with Luke. If she told him that, she figured that Luke might think it was true and that was the last thing she needed. "Could we talk about something else?"

He shrugged. "Sure." He gestured toward the books. "Did you want to take a break?"

"Yes." She studied Luke as he got up from the table and poured himself a glass of water. He was just so….different than what she remembered. He was so nice, kind, and polite. It was like, he was the same, but, different, if that made any sense. His devotion toward his daughter seemed to soften him a bit, making him not so rough around the edges. He returned to the table, caught her staring at him. She swallowed, slightly embarrassed that he'd caught her ogling him. She cleared her throat. "Can I ask you something?"

"Sure. But before you do that, I want to thank you again. You don't know how much it means to me that you've taken time to study with me tonight."

"Did it help?"

"Yes, but…"

"I know. We didn't get through all of the points that you wanted to go over."

He nodded. "I'm going to need your help. I could pay you if you want."

Paying for her tutoring services? It just sounded a bit weird. "No, you don't have to pay me. If I ever need a favor, I'll keep you in mind, okay?"

He smiled. "Okay. Now, what did you want to

ask me?"

"I know you'd mentioned that Salina had died, but I was wondering what happened?" She paused. "My mom died of cancer not too long ago. That's one of the reasons why I came home."

He sighed, leaned back into his chair. "I know about your mom. I read the obituary online. I was sorry to hear about her passing. I prayed for you and your dad when I found out."

This was a surprise. "You were looking up my mom online?"

He told her how he'd happened to Google her. His only intent was to see if she'd changed since high school. "I told you that I go overboard where Lisa is concerned. She's going to a slumber party next Saturday. I've already gone to the house and met the parents, asked them questions. I know they probably think I'm weird, but, I'm concerned about who spends time with my daughter. Besides, she's never spent the night away from home."

Lisa had never spent the night away from home? That was so strange.

"Anyway, about Salina, she was killed in a car accident a year ago."

She touched his hand. "I'm sorry."

He barely nodded, accepting her apology. "I was living near my cousins, and they curse, drink a lot, some of them do drugs. I didn't want Lisa exposed to that. They were always coming to my house, and it just got too complicated. I figured it was time for me to move away from them. I wanted a wholesome environment for my daughter so I recalled how Bethlehem was a small, nice town. I found a job in the area and Lisa and I relocated here."

He continued telling her about what his life had been like after he'd left Bethlehem. "When I first left Bethlehem, my mom had been unemployed and she'd found a job a few hours away." He took a sip from his water glass. "When we'd decided to move, my mom agreed to take Salina with us. She'd just turned eighteen and she was in foster care. Her foster parents weren't going to let her stay since they were no longer going to get paid for her care since she was eighteen. My mom felt responsible for her because she was pregnant with her grandchild."

She'd forgotten that Salina was a foster kid. She still wondered why he'd chosen to be with Salina instead of her, why he'd cheated on her with Salina. She also wondered why he'd left without saying good-bye. Her dad's conversation still hovered in her mind and she didn't think it was wise to tell Luke how much he'd hurt her when he'd left all those years ago.

He told of dropping out of high school, getting his GED, marrying Salina, staying close to his extended family since they often offered emotional and financial support.

"What about your mom? Did you stay close to her?"

He shook his head. "My mom eventually remarried and she lives with her new husband in Florida. Anyway, about a year before Salina's car accident, we started going to church. Both of us joined a church, and accepted Christ. You know, things aren't always perfect, but, telling God about my problems makes me feel a heck of a lot better."

Kim nodded, blessed by Luke's faith journey. She

glanced at the clock, startled that it was midnight! They'd been talking for three hours! She yawned. "Well, I'd better be heading home. My dad will wonder where I've been." It was still kind of hard for her to get used to living with her dad. He still treated her like she was in high school, and she could imagine him waiting up for her, getting ready to give her the third degree because she'd been out so late. Why couldn't her dad treat her like a grown woman, instead of a wild teenager who'd stayed out late past her curfew? Luke touched her face, the warmth from his fingers skittered across her skin. She resisted the urge to take his hand, find solace from his gentle touch.

"Are you okay? You looked upset."

"Just thinking about my dad."

Luke frowned, but, didn't comment as he got her coat, helped her put it on. When they stepped outside, Kim giggled when she spotted freshly-fallen snow. Several houses had Christmas lights winking in the inky darkness. "Luke, it's so beautiful out here," she breathed, raising her face to the sky, feeling the cold flakes of snow on her skin. Rarely did they see snow during the Christmas season in Bethlehem. As she stepped down onto the sidewalk, her foot hit an icy patch and she slipped. Luke caught her in his arms and when his warm lips lightly pressed against her mouth, her heart skipped a beat.

"Kim I couldn't resist. This snow is not nearly as beautiful as you are." Speechless, Kim didn't know what to say. He walked her to her car, opened the door for her. "Call me when you get home so that I know you arrived safely."

She mutely nodded, starting the ignition.

CHAPTER 5

THE ECHO OF SLEIGH BELLS, Christmas music and partying filled the air as Kim opened the door of her cookie shop. She grinned as the Christmas parade with the fire engine carrying Santa Claus headed down Main Street. Watching the Christmas parade had been something she'd enjoyed doing with her mother every year. This was the first year that she'd watched the festivities without her mom and a sudden sinking, bittersweet feeling settled into her gut. As the high school marching band strutted by, the majorettes twirled their batons into the air, and their white boots clattered against the frigid street, as they performed their routine. Kim's euphoria evaporated and she sighed.

Since her mom had passed, she'd found that she could get sad at any moment. Puffs of white air escaped from her mouth into the cold air, and she took another deep breath, fisting her hands. Tears rushed to her eyes and she blinked, unable to keep the moisture from spilling from her eyes. Her mom had loved watching the marching bands in the parade. A musician, her mom had grown up playing the flute and had been in the marching band when she'd been in high school. She had also played with the church praise and worship band until she'd been too sick to participate.

Lisa tugged her hand, pulling her out of her reverie. "What's the matter Ms. Kim?"

Kim glanced down at Lisa, her heart tugging with pride. Lisa had proven to be a huge asset to their bakery, and she loved helping serve the customers. Although today was Saturday, Luke had asked if it was okay if Kim stayed the entire day at the cookie shop since he was meeting with some of his friends from the college for an all-day study session. He'd initially wanted to leave Lisa with a sitter, but, Lisa had begged him to let her work with Kim for the entire day.

She pulled the girl into a hug, breathing in her refreshing little-girl scent of soap and lotion. "I'm just missing my mom." She released Lisa, looked into the child's intelligent, dark-brown eyes.

"Dad told me that your mom's dead, too." The child paused, bit her lower lip. Right now, she looked so much like her father that it tugged at Kim's heart. When she'd initially spotted Lisa, two weeks ago, at the Career Day event, she had not noticed the resemblance between Luke and his daughter. However, now, she did see some resemblance between them. "I miss my mom, too. Sometimes, I cry when I miss her a lot."

Kim hugged Lisa again, unsure of what to tell the child to make the pain better. Sure, she could mention that both of their mothers were in heaven, but, that did little to minimize the daily pain felt from losing a parent. Kim rubbed her eyes, figuring young Lisa had it rougher than she did. Lisa was just a little girl, and every little girl needed a mom.

The parade ended and confetti scattered the road as the last float made the trek down the street. Kim tugged Lisa into the warm cookie shop, the scents of vanilla and peppermint floated through the air. During Christmas, they always made their special peppermint cookies. Kim had made a batch that morning, before Lisa had arrived. Kim's father had been complaining about a sore throat that morning, so, he wasn't working in the cookie shop that day. She'd gotten him some cold medicine and, last she'd checked, he'd been sleeping soundly.

As customers strolled into the shop, she thought about all that had happened over the last week. Since Luke had kissed her during the snowfall one week ago, things had been weird and stilted between them. She'd immediately texted her friends, Heather, Carly and Anna, as soon as she'd arrived home from last Saturday's study session, telling them about kissing Luke. She'd even met her friend Heather for coffee. Heather had advised Kim to take things slow, one day at a time. She'd also told Kim that she needed to get to know Luke again since it'd been eight years since he'd left Bethlehem.

Heather had also been discussing their annual cookie sleepover that happened every Christmas. Every year, since they were kids, Kim, Heather, Anna, and Carly had gotten together for a sleepover every Christmas, and they'd also brought cookies to exchange. Due to scheduling conflicts, they'd decided to have the cookie sleepover on the day after Christmas at Kim's house.

All of these thoughts tumbled through her mind. She went into the back of the kitchen and placed a pan of her famous vanilla cookies into the oven and set the timer. As she prepared more cookie dough, the acrid scent of smoke filled the kitchen. Lisa rushed into the kitchen. "Ms. Kim, what's wrong?" Kim coughed, pulling the burned pan of cookies from the oven. She checked the timer, confused. These cookies still had four minutes left to bake, and they'd burned to a crisp! Her precious cookies looked like black hockey pucks!

She dumped the cookies into the garbage can, turned the oven off, before rushing to the front of the shop. Customers were covering their noses, coughing. "Sorry. My oven is broken." Only a few cookies were left in the display case. It looked like she'd be closing early.

Luke slammed his Calculus book shut. His study group had left the library and he was the only one left behind. They were going out for pizza, and Luke's stomach growled. He'd wanted to join them, but, figured his time would be better spent going over everything they'd discussed during their day-long study session. Derivatives, integrals, equations, graphs…all of this was balled up into his mind like a massive tangled mass. He'd been in deep trouble in Calculus before Kim had started tutoring him. Although he wasn't totally up to par on his Calculus, he was in a somewhat better position than he was before Kim had started helping him.

He swallowed, lowered his head into the crook of his arms as he leaned across the desk. He breathed deeply. He really needed to calm himself down. Over the past week, whenever he felt anxious about his math class, he'd stop, and think about the amazing kiss he'd shared with Kim. When their lips had touched, long dormant feelings had slammed into him like the speed of a freight truck. Memories of being with Kim, laughing with her, eating warm cookies and milk…arguing. They'd argued a lot when they were dating in high school, but, both of them had been young, immature, and they'd had their share of problems. He'd wondered what would happen if he asked Kim if they could date, like a couple. Would she agree?

Since they'd kissed, she'd been wary, almost as if she'd been sorry that they'd kissed on that cold, snowy night. She continued tutoring him, and he could tell that she struggled to stay on the subject of math. Something was bothering her, and he'd asked what was wrong, but, she'd said that everything was fine. It'd been on the tip of his tongue to tell her that he was sorry he kissed her, but, frankly, he wasn't sorry.

It was against his beliefs to lie, so, he wasn't going to apologize for kissing her. The kiss had been wonderful, and he'd enjoyed it. He'd enjoyed it so much that he wanted to do it again. "Lord, what can I do?" He glanced around the group study section of the community college library. A few students sat at the tables, poring over books, some had their laptops open, typing.

He needed to pass this class. He needed a degree

so that he could provide a better life for Lisa. He didn't want to just rent his home, he wanted to own his own home one day, making the salary that he wanted. From his research, the only way to make the amount of money he needed in his profession was to get his bachelor's degree. Getting his Associates' degree from Bethlehem Community College was just the first step to a better way of life.

Passing this class was just part of the first step.

He checked his watch, his stomach growling again. He really needed to get going so that he could fetch Lisa and take her to her friend's house. One of her school mates was hosting a birthday slumber party this evening, and she needed to be there in an hour. They'd packed her sleeping bag and her other things before he'd dropped her off at Kim's that morning. All he needed to do was pick her up and drop her off at her friend's house. Apparently, they'd be serving pizza, cake and punch for dinner at the slumber party.

He glanced at his book again. He needed to study this evening. Would Kim be willing to help him study tonight? They didn't have a study session planned but, if she didn't have plans, then he wondered… No, he couldn't ask her to do that for him. He was already taking advantage of her time and to ask her to help him tonight….he just didn't want to impose. His cell phone buzzed. He checked the Caller ID, spotting Kim's number at the cookie bakery. "Hey, Kim."

"Dad, it's me, not Kim. Where are you? I don't want to be late."

He chuckled, shoving his Calculus book into his backpack. "I'm on my way."

"Good. Ms. Kim is mad because the cookies burned."

He frowned. "Huh?"

Before he could comment further, his daughter disconnected the call.

CHAPTER 6

LUKE PULLED INTO AN EMPTY parking space in front of the bakery. The CLOSED sign was posted on the door and he walked in, the sleigh bells above the entrance tinkling. Kim and Lisa sat at a table, apparently waiting for him. Kim's brow puckered with worry and the acrid smell of burnt food filled the air. The scent reminded him of his burned dinners. "Dad, we need to get going!" Lisa rushed to him, holding her overnight bag.

"We'll leave in a minute." He focused on Kim. "You burned your cookies?" He couldn't recall Kim ever burning cookies, not even when they'd been in high school.

She shook her head. "No, the oven's broken."

"Did you call the repair man?"

She nodded. "I did but, they'd already closed for the day. I probably won't be able to get an appointment until Monday."

Finally, he'd found a way to help Kim! "I can probably fix it for you."

"Really?"

He'd found that over the years, he was pretty

handy at fixing things. Sometimes, he'd had to use the internet and look at YouTube videos for instructions, but, if he focused, he was usually able to fix just about any appliance or plumbing problem. When he'd been married to Salina, they'd not had much money, but, they'd never had to call a repair man since Luke was always able to figure out how to fix their appliances.

Kim sounded so surprised that he'd wondered if she thought he was a loser. After all, he couldn't cook, he was terrible at math, and he was at odds as to what to do with his daughter. His life was a mess, and she probably regretted kissing him one week ago. "I can try. I'll drop off Lisa and be right back."

His daughter settled into the back seat of the car, pulled out our IPod, placed her earbuds into her ears, listening to her music. While driving, he prayed, unsure what to do about his budding feelings for Kim. *Lord, I liked kissing Kim. I'm attracted to her. But, I don't know what to do about it. Do you think I should talk to her about it, Lord? What can I do?*

He pulled on to the street in front of the home where the slumber party was being held. He dropped off Lisa, making sure she had all of her stuff, including the festive pink gift bag containing her birthday present. As he waved goodbye and got back into his car, he realized this would be the first evening he'd had alone, without Lisa, since she'd been born. He returned to Kim's bakery, pulled into the open space in front of the establishment. Gripping the steering wheel, he hesitated, closed his eyes. *Be truthful. Talk to her.* The words came clear and strong into his mind as he got out of the car, and strolled to the bakery.

Kim waited for him, her dark eyes wary. Her dad's tool box rested on the table. She looked so upset that all he wanted to do was pull her into his arms, kiss her full, pouty lips. But, he couldn't do that now. She obviously didn't want his affection. He made himself comfortable at the table, removing his phone from his pocket. Kim sat beside him, her brow furrowed as he went onto the internet, searching. The pleasant floral scent of her perfume teased his nose, again reminding him about how attractive she was. "Now, what's wrong with your oven again?"

Kim's mouth dropped open. "Don't you have to look at the oven to see? Why are you looking at your cell phone?"

He resisted the urge to groan. He took a deep breath, again recalling that they were not as well acquainted as they should be. Since their passionate kiss, she'd been doing a good job of keeping emotionally distant. After he fixed her oven, they were going to have a serious discussion about that. "Look, I'm good at fixing things. You don't remember how I'd fixed that old motorcycle in high school?"

When they were teens, he had not had much money, but he'd wanted a motorcycle. He'd worked and was able to purchase a used motorcycle that needed a lot of work. He'd discovered his knack for fixing not only bikes, but, cars, too. "Before I work on an appliance, I usually look on the internet first, look at YouTube videos, to see how to fix a problem. It doesn't take me too long and I'm usually able to fix it."

She raised one of her cute, thick eyebrows. "Usually?"

Did she think he wouldn't be able to help her? "What happened to your oven?"

She sighed. "My cookies burn, even if I set the timer. They burn after only a few minutes."

"Sounds like the heating element is out." After doing his research, he returned the phone to his pocket. "Let me see your oven." He followed her back to the kitchen, trying to ignore the cute sway of her hips as she made her way toward the oven. He opened it, looked inside. After he was finished, he told her what he needed. "I can buy the stuff at the appliance store." He checked his watch. "They should still be open."

After they'd purchased what was needed and he'd done the repair, Kim pulled out some cookie dough. "I want to test the oven to be sure it's working." His stomach growled as she plopped the cookie dough onto the pan, about to place it into the pre-heated oven.

"Hungry?"

"Yes." He didn't bother telling her that he'd declined the dinner invite from his study group since he'd wanted to spend an extra hour studying. Soon, the scent of chocolate chip cookies filled the air. Kim pulled out her cell phone and ordered a large pizza. Surprisingly, she'd ordered his favorite toppings: pepperoni, mushroom, and onion. During their high school dates, they'd often eaten pizza at the pizza parlor. He had to wonder if she ordered that kind of pizza because she'd remembered it was what he liked.

Soon the pizza had been delivered. Luke payed

the delivery man and Kim boxed up the cookies that she'd just baked. "Let's go to the house to eat." She locked the door to the bakery and they walked the few steps to Kim's home, which was adjacent to the bakery. They entered the festive yellow kitchen, and again memories bombarded him. He'd spent a lot of time in this house, usually when Kim's parents were out.

The same rooster-patterned wallpaper lined the perimeter of the room. They sat at the table and he took her hand and prayed over their meal. They then consumed the pizza, guzzling ice-cold Cokes. Once they were done with their meal, Luke leaned back against his seat, focused on Kim. A drop of pizza sauce stained the side of her mouth. He leaned toward her, swiped the stray sauce away. Her pretty eyes widened, and she looked at him.

He shrugged. "Sorry. I couldn't resist."

After they'd feasted on chocolate chip cookies and cold milk for dessert, Luke broached the subject of his Calculus. He told her about his studying in the library for the day. "I just need to go over some of the concepts they covered today."

They moved to the living room and Luke pulled out his book and after about an hour of studying, he finally felt he spotted a light at the end of the tunnel of darkness of Calculus. He took a deep breath, the quietness surrounding them. He glanced around Kim's familiar living room. He'd spent a lot of time in Kim's small house. He recalled knocking on her window in the middle of the night so that he could sneak into her room. At one point, her parents had forbidden her to date him, which was when they'd started secretly meeting behind her parents' backs, which had been blatantly wrong. Since he was a parent now, looking back on his life, he knew that Kim's parents only had her best interests at heart. He was a wild, reckless teen and her parents were only trying to protect her. Whenever he was with Kim, he seemed to be caught in a vicious cycle of thinking about the past.

He needed to think about now, right now. There was so much about Kim that he didn't know, and all he could do to start things off, remove this awkwardness between them, would be to be honest with her. "I can't stop thinking about that kiss." There, he'd said it. He'd opened up the conversation and it would be up to Kim to help him carry this through. If she didn't like the kiss, then, she could confess that to him, let him know. At that point, he'd at least make an effort to stop these kissing fantasies before they got out of hand.

Her brown skin flushed, and she raised her eyebrows. He waited. He could wait all night if he had to. But, they needed to clear the air, discuss this apparent attraction between them. He didn't want any interruptions, either.

"Where's your dad?"

She swallowed, scratched the back of her neck. Did his confession surprise her, make her feel uneasy? "He's asleep. I think he's catching a cold or something."

He nodded, glad to hear that their conversation probably wouldn't be interrupted. "Kim, we really need to talk."

"Talk? Do you mean about the kiss?"

He nodded, scooting closer towards her. He wanted to take her into his arms, kiss her again, but, he tightened his hands into fists, refusing to touch her until they'd cleared the air. "I liked kissing you. I liked it so much that whenever I feel overwhelmed about my math, I think about kissing you and I calm down."

She raised her eyebrows, cleared her throat. "I liked kissing you, too."

This was good to hear. Now they were getting somewhere. "Since we kissed, we've been awkward and uneasy toward each other."

She nodded. "I wasn't sure if us kissing was a good idea."

"Why?"

"My life is a mess. I'm unemployed and that's why I moved back home to help with the cookie bakery."

He shrugged. "Why would being unemployed make your life a mess? I don't care if you have a job."

"Well, I care. I don't know if I want to stay here in Bethlehem with my dad."

Whoa, this was a surprise. He'd just assumed she was comfortable working in the cookie bakery again. "So, we can discuss that later. But, why do you say your life is a mess? Is it just because you're not using your college degree?"

She bit her lower lip, looked toward the wall. "No," she mumbled. She was hiding something. He could feel it. Kim never looked you in the eye when she didn't want to talk about something. She finally turned to face him again. "I honestly didn't know if the kiss was just nostalgic, or, if it really meant something to you."

"You say nostalgic. I guess you're talking about

when we were kids."

She nodded. "I keep thinking about the past."

He nodded. "Me too. But, you know, we need to get to know each other as we are now. We shouldn't use the past to judge our relationship now."

She frowned. "What relationship?"

"There's so much about you that I don't know. I want to spend time with you. I'm not just talking about your helping me to study either."

She blinked, as if she found his words stunning. "Do you mean date?"

He nodded. "Yes. I think the Lord used Lisa to bring us together."

She scoffed. "You sound like Heather."

"Heather? Are you talking about your friend from high school?"

She folded her arms in front of her chest. "Yes. She basically told me the same thing."

"Sounds like Heather knows what she's talking about." He recalled the rip in his backpack that caused his Calculus book to tumble out while he'd been in her bakery. "Maybe He brought us together so that you could help me with my math. But, maybe something more. We'll never know unless we try."

"Luke, I don't know. So much has happened…" The distress in her voice made him pause. Unable to resist, he took her hand.

"What do you mean?"

She chewed on her lower lip. "Look, I was engaged and it ended badly, right after the holidays last year. I lost my job…"

He caressed her fingers. "What happened with your job?"

Luke held her hand as she told him about her years in college, getting her accounting degree, passing the CPA exam. She then told him about having her first job out of college and being laid off four years later. She gave no details about her big breakup with her boyfriend during Christmas last year. He wasn't sure if she wanted to avoid the subject, or, if she simply forgot to talk about it. He made a mental note to ask her about that later. "Luke, I just thought I was so great. I knew layoffs were coming, but, I honestly didn't think anything like that would happen to me." She then told of her mom's death, and about how it had affected her. "So, I figured since I was unemployed and my mom had passed, I may as well move back home and be with dad. He needed my help."

Her voice faltered when she mentioned her father. "You don't get along with your dad?"

She shrugged. "About as well as we can. He doesn't agree with everything that I do."

"When you mention him, you seem upset. Why move back in with him if he upsets you?"

She looked at him as if he were an idiot. She raised her right eyebrow, an old habit she used to have when she was mad. "Because he needs my help, that's why."

"That first night you helped me study?"

"Yes?"

"You'd said that your dad was glad to hear from Tina?"

He'd never understood why Kim felt inferior to her sibling. She'd often told him that Tina was the favored sibling in the family, but, he'd never witnessed this. The times he'd spent with Kim's family, he had not noticed any favoritism, but, perhaps he was not able to notice that since he'd been a young, self-centered teen at the time. The few times he'd run into Kim's dad, when he'd come to get Lisa, her dad would give him a cool nod, maybe a hello. He had not been overly friendly, but, he did seem to dote on Lisa.

Kim scoffed. "You'd think that Tina hung the moon the way my dad gushes when she calls. If he's in a bad mood, then talking to Tina makes him feel better." She shrugged. "I'm here, helping out with the family business, and my presence doesn't seem to bring him much joy."

He continued holding her warm hand, the distress in her voice making him pause. "Can I be honest with you about something?"

She leaned back, her eyes widening. "You must be planning on telling me something big if you say that."

He blew air through his lips, not wanting her to lose her temper. But, being honest was what he was all about nowadays. If what he said made Kim angry, then he'd simply apologize and try not to upset her again. "I don't think you moved back home because you were unemployed and you'd broken up with your ex. I don't even think you came back to help your dad."

She jerked her hand away. "You don't know a whole lot about me and my life."

This was going to be harder than he thought. "I know that, but, I'm trying to learn. I like you, Kim, and I hate to see you hurting."

"I'm not hurting."

"Yes you are." He touched her shoulder. *Lord,*

please don't let her lose her temper. "It sounds like you moved back home to try and get your dad to like you better."

She furrowed her cute brow, chewed her lower lip. "What do you mean?"

He took a deep breath. "Kim, you've always envied the relationship your father had with Tina. You want the same kind of relationship. You moved back home to try and make your father love you as much as he loves Tina."

Her eyes widened and she scooted away from him. Wow, looked like he'd made her really mad. He touched her shoulder, desperately wanting to calm her down. "Honey, don't get upset."

"Don't call me honey," she said through clenched teeth. "Are you implying that I moved back home just to get my dad's approval? Do you know how pathetic that sounds?"

She'd raised her voice. She'd always gotten loud when she was angry. He calmed her down the only way he knew how. He leaned toward her, pressed his lips to hers. She tasted good and sweet, like chocolate and vanilla.

"What's going on in here?" Kim's dad, James Taylor, stomped into the living room, staring at them with his groggy-looking eyes. He wore his bathrobe and Luke figured Kim's loud voice had woken him up. Maybe it was time for him to go home.

CHAPTER 7

"**WHY ARE YOU BAKING COOKIES?**" Her dad came into the kitchen, his hands shoved into the pockets of his bathrobe.

Still mad about the previous night, Kim didn't initially respond. She pulled the pan of heart-shaped vanilla cookies from the oven. It was Sunday and the bakery was closed, but, she'd had a sleepless night and had wanted to *do* something. She'd attended a sunrise service at church before going for a long, hard run. With longing, she recalled that she and Luke had gone running together as part of their Physical Education class in school. Luke had been pretty fast and she'd always struggled to keep up with him. He'd slowed his pace for her, and she'd often wondered why he'd never gone out for the track and field team at school.

Luke. Luke. Luke. He'd popped into her mind yet again and it was driving her crazy. They'd not had time to finish their conversation last night since her dad interrupted them. Luke had boldly apologized to her father before making his exit. Her father had then bombarded her with questions, his deep voice sounding gruff from his cold. Upset about what Luke had said, and unable to talk to her father without losing her temper, she'd mumbled that she was going to bed.

She'd baked these cookies to take to the homeless shelter. At church, the pastor had said that the local homeless shelter had been lacking with funds. She'd given money for the special collection they'd taken on the shelter's behalf. After church, she'd contacted the shelter and offered to bring cookies. The shelter director had been delighted, stating that they seldom had desserts to give to their guests.

She'd also wanted to take some of these cookies over to Luke so that they could finish last night's conversation, but, she didn't think it was a good idea to just barge over to his place on a Sunday morning, bearing a hot plate of cookies. She had no idea where he worshipped and she knew that Lisa was going to be at the slumber party until after lunch, so, she figured she'd have a chance to talk to him alone.

"Kim, do you hear me talking to you?"

"Yes, Dad." Taking a spatula, she slid it underneath a cookie, setting it on a cooling rack. She continued her chore, explaining about the homeless shelter. "So, I'm going to be heading over there shortly." Her dad still sounded like he had a cold, but, he did sound a bit better. "How are you feeling?"

He shrugged. "Just a cold. Will be gone soon. Look, about Luke—"

"I don't want to talk about Luke." Luke was none of her dad's business. She was an adult now, not some wild teenager who refused to listen to her parents. She could make her own decisions.

"Now, listen to me, Little Girl, I'm your father. I'm older than you and I know more about these things than you do."

Kim rolled her eyes, plopping the dough for another batch of vanilla cookies onto the cookie sheet. She performed her chore quickly, before shoving the pan into the hot oven. She resisted the urge to yell and scream at her dad. Luke had hinted about their dating last night, if she understood him correctly. If she did date him, officially, what would her dad think? She'd spent half the night thinking about what Luke had said about her moving back home, desperate to gain her father's approval. Was she really that desperate to gain her father's love?

"Maybe you need to talk to Tina about this. She always knew how to pick respectable men to date."

"Dad, stop it already!" Her voice rang throughout the warm kitchen and her dad backed away a few steps, his dark eyes widening.

"How dare you raise your voice at me?"

Kim swallowed, suddenly filled with shame. She had not yelled at her father like that since she'd been a wild, rebellious teenager. Anger and fury filled her soul. Hot tears coursed down her cheeks and she brushed the moisture away. More tears came and before she knew it she cried, howling. Her shoulders shook and she finally plopped into the kitchen chair. Her dad's shuffling feet sounded behind her and he sat at the table with her. He pulled her into his arms, and Kim cried into his bathrobe, sniffing the familiar aromatic scent of his lime aftershave. She cried for several minutes and when the oven timer buzzed, she put her oven mitts on and removed the pan of hot cookies from the oven. She didn't bother placing them on the cooling rack. She returned to the table where her dad patiently sat, waiting for her.

She dropped into a chair, consumed with exhaustion. Her sleepless night was catching up to her. Last night, Luke had mentioned being honest and open, well, that's what she was going to do right now. She was going to be honest with her dad and then, she would go visit Luke before she took her vanilla cookies to the homeless shelter. She took deep breaths, blew her nose, and forced herself to calm down. She needed to clear the air with her father, that's what she needed to do.

Her dad cleared his throat, leaned back into the chair, and folded his arms in front of him. "Are you going to tell me what all that crying was about?"

She nodded, folded her hands in front of her. Lord, help her. She really needed God's help right now. "Dad, I hate it when you do that."

"Do what?" He raised his hands into the air, as if he were surrendering after a battle.

"I hate it when you compare me to Tina. Why on earth would I call Tina to ask about dating Luke?"

"Are you seriously dating Luke Barnes?" Her dad stood up, his hands balled into fists.

She needed to stay focused. This conversation would be going nowhere if they kept changing topics. "This isn't about Luke. This is about you, me, and Tina."

He shrugged, returned to his chair. "Well, what about us?"

"Dad, I hate it when you compare me to Tina. You make it seem like Tina is so great, and I'm just an afterthought."

"What?" Her dad seemed truly puzzled. She really had to spell this out for him.

"When Tina calls you, it makes you happy. Tina is married to a doctor. She has a nice perfect family. You think Tina's life is perfect and you think my life stinks."

"Whoa. Little Girl, you're way off base—"

"No, I'm not. When Tina calls you, you get in a better mood. When I'm here and when I used to call you, you never sounded as happy as when you talk to Tina. You always have something negative to say to me. Not once have you told me that you were grateful about my moving back home to help with the bakery. I'm starting to wonder if you even want me here."

Her father scooted toward her, took her hand. "Honey, I want you here, with me. But I don't want you to stay unless you really want to. I know you have your degree and all and sooner or later, you'll probably return to your accounting profession." He paused, continued holding her hands. "I just have a hard time...well, you used to be so wild, making bad decisions. Tina was never like that."

"Tina's made mistakes too Dad and you know it." Her words were met with silence. "But you seem to think that Tina's a better person than me, and it hurts me when you imply that Tina is better." When Tina had gone away to college, she'd gotten her first serious boyfriend. She'd gotten pregnant, but, she'd suffered a late-term miscarriage. The family never spoke about that awful time, and she'd always felt that her dad had simply swept it under the rug, as if it never happened, not wanting to recall that Tina wasn't so perfect after all.

When her dad sat there, mute, Kim figured he wasn't going to say anything. "I'm going to box up my cookies to take to the homeless shelter." She stood up.

"Little Girl. Wait." She stopped, paused, before she returned to the table. "Maybe I do act as if Tina is better, but, it's not for the reasons that you think."

"Well, why then?"

He paused before he stood up. "I'll be right back." He returned a few minutes later with an old, battered photo album.

Kim frowned, staring at the cracked leather. "I've never seen that before."

"It's up in my bedroom. I don't take it out too much." He opened it, pointed to an old picture. "That's Tina."

Kim leaned forward to get a closer look at the child. The child looked exactly like Tina. "This can't be Tina, Dad, this picture is too old."

He shook his head. "I don't mean your sister Tina. That's Tina, my sister."

"You have a sister?" Kim swallowed, stunned. "Dad, you never mentioned her before."

"She died when she was eleven. Had problems with her heart. We were so close. It's still hard for me to talk about her. When Tina, your sister, was born, well, that's why I named her Tina, after my dead sister. I then noticed how much she looked like Tina, she even walks and sounds like my sister." He sniffed, and Kim realized her dad was crying. He dried his tears on the sleeve of his tattered robe. "Just reminds me of the sister that I lost is all. Tina does." He sighed. "I don't talk about my dead sister because it hurts. I see that my reaction to Tina bothers you, hurts you, Little Girl, and that makes me sad. There's so much about you that makes me proud."

This was a surprise. "Really? Like what?"

He sighed, wiped his wet eyes. "I'm proud that you're a CPA. I'm proud that you were out there in Chicago, that big city, living on your own. Tina was always kind of delicate to me. I'd never imagine her striking out in the big city like you. You were always tougher than your sister." He cleared his throat. "From now on, I'll make sure that I'm more sensitive about how I treat the both of you. Both you and Tina are my girls and I love both of you." He paused, took her hand. "Now, about Luke."

"Oh, Dad." She didn't want to talk about Luke. She needed to let her dad know about what she'd been through almost one year ago. "Do you remember when I was dating Bill? I'd mentioned him to you and mom last Christmas."

Her father nodded. "Yeah, I remember your mentioning him, but you never brought him home with you." He shrugged. "You'd said that things didn't work out between the two of you."

"Well, what I failed to tell you was that I was engaged to him."

"Engaged?" Her dad raised his eyebrows, leaned back into his chair.

Instead of talking about her feelings for Luke, they spent the next hour, Kim openly telling her dad about her brief engagement last Christmas, and about how it had all ended so suddenly.

CHAPTER 8

LUKE SPED PAST THE OAK tree, revving his motorcycle. The cold wind whipped around him, and he had to really struggle to maintain the speed limit. He left his neighborhood, riding onto the main road before entering the highway. Revving his engine, he let loose, going as fast as he was allowed on the open road. It was an early Sunday morning and traffic was light on the main highway.

Since Lisa was away at her slumber party, he'd had the luxury of enjoying a Sunday morning motorcycle ride. He'd overslept and missed church, but, he'd spent some quiet time with the Lord that morning, praying about his situation with Kim. After riding for an hour, he finally returned to Bethlehem, and minutes later, he pulled onto his familiar street. He passed the corner of his street, his house was just ahead. He breathed deeply, white puffs of breath coming from his mouth in the frigid cold air. Since it was cloudy, several people had turned on their Christmas lights and the multi-colored bulbs winked in the cloudy day.

A car pulled to his curb. He glanced over and

spotted Kim's vehicle. Hopefully, she wasn't still mad at him about what he'd said about her relationship with her dad. He parked his bike, removed his helmet, before walking toward Kim's car. He opened her door for her.

She looked pretty, refreshing. But, she also looked tired. Dark circles were beneath her eyes, and her hair was pulled back into a sleek ponytail. "Thanks for opening the door for me."

He nodded. "You're welcome." At least she didn't appear to be mad at him anymore.

She reached over to the passenger seat and removed a box. He sniffed. Smelled like cookies. He could use a snack right now. He didn't have to pick up Lisa for a few hours, so, they could relax and finish the conversation they'd started the previous night.

She gave him the box, exited the car before slamming her door shut. She remained silent, so, he gestured toward the house. "Come on in." They walked to his door and he unlocked it. He went into the kitchen, set the box on the table. Kim glanced at the carton of eggs and the pack of bacon he'd left on the counter. "Looks like you were about to cook breakfast."

He chuckled. "More like I was going to try to make breakfast food for lunch. I love bacon, but, I always burn it. I can make scrambled eggs if I concentrate. Lisa said my scrambled eggs look more brown than yellow."

She hesitated, touched the carton of eggs and the package of bacon. "I haven't had lunch yet. Do you mind if I fixed the food and we ate together?" She didn't look at him when she asked, just kept staring at the carton of eggs. She seemed nervous, and he figured she might feel bad for yelling at him the previous night. It was hard to tell.

"I don't mind." As a matter of fact, he felt like getting down on his knees and thanking God for answering his prayer. He'd been worried about Kim all night, but, had hesitated to call. He figured he wouldn't be seeing her again until he went to pick up Lisa at the bakery the next day.

Kim pulled out his big frying pan and minutes later, the delicious, meaty scent of bacon filled the kitchen. He started a pot of coffee, removed milk and juice from the refrigerator. He set the bowl of sugar on the table. Both of them remained silent, but, it was more a silence of comfort. For some reason, Luke figured Kim wanted to talk about something, but, she'd start talking when she was ready. After he'd placed everything on the table, including toast with butter, he sat down, watched Kim's shapely backside as she fried the meat.

Goodness, she was beautiful. Just seeing her in his warm kitchen, making him a meal…filled him with happiness. He could get used to seeing her every night, making dinner in his kitchen. He honestly didn't know if she'd be open to having a relationship with him, but, he certainly hoped she'd at least let him try. His attraction to her proved too strong to ignore, and he didn't know if she shared his deep feelings.

She placed napkins onto a plate and put the cooked bacon onto the napkins so that the grease could drain from the meat. After she'd scrambled their eggs, he stood and got the bacon, brought it to the table. She soon followed with the plate of cooked eggs. They bowed their heads, and he took her hand, caressed her fingers. Still nervous, he wanted to be sure he prayed before his meal, as he usually did, but, wanted her to know that he wanted the Lord to intervene, make her feel better. He cleared this throat, still holding her hand. "Lord, please be with Kim. I know she was upset last night and I just want her to feel better. I want her to be happy Lord. Thank you for this meal that You've provided for us and thanks Lord, for Kim's company. It was a blessing when she showed up at my door this morning. Amen."

"Amen."

He released her hand and they dug into the food. They ate silently, and Luke gobbled his food, thinking the last time he'd had a meal that tasted this good was when he'd taken Lisa out to breakfast at the Waffle House a few weeks ago. After they'd finished consuming their meal, they sipped coffee. Kim opened up her box of cookies and the delicious scent of vanilla floated from the box. He took one of the thin, crisp, heart-shaped cookies, bit into it. The taste of vanilla exploded into his mouth and he gobbled two cookies before focusing on his coffee. "Those cookies are good."

"Thanks. It's my mom's recipe. I think about her whenever I make them."

Once they'd finished with their coffee and cookies, Luke beckoned Kim into the living room. He raised the blinds. The day remained cloudy and the Christmas lights continued blinking from the homes across the street. He sat beside her on the couch, resisting the urge to hold her hand. He figured she was probably ready to talk. "I'm sorry for yelling at you last night."

He nodded. "I was worried about you."

She blinked, looked at him, her dark eyes apprehensive. "You were?"

"Yes. What did your father say after I left?"

She told him about the conversation she'd had with her father that morning. The news was stunning. "When he told me about his dead sister, I was shocked."

"I'm shocked. At least it explains why he seems to favor Tina over you." He paused, not sure if he should mention this, but, felt he needed to know. "Do you think your relationship with your father will change now?"

She chewed her lower lip, glancing at the Christmas lights winking from the homes across the street. "I think so. I'm not saying that things will be perfect, but, I think things will be better."

"Thank God for that."

"I also wanted you to talk to you about us seeing each other."

"You mean dating?" She nodded. Her pretty mouth drooped with sadness. "Kim, why are you so sad? You don't want to spend time with me?" If she didn't want to date him, then he would simply need to understand and move on with his life. It would be difficult for him to do since Kim constantly dominated his thoughts, haunting his dreams.

"I'm concerned about how things ended between us eight years ago."

"Whoa, Honey, don't go there. We were both young, immature, and we didn't know the Lord back then."

She shook her head, looked directly at him. "In spite of all that, I need to know why you left me eight years ago without even saying good bye. I looked for you, couldn't find you. I was hurting for a long time before I forced myself to realize that our relationship meant nothing to you."

"Kim, I'm so sorry."

"I don't want your apology. I just want to know what happened. Before I agree to date you, this is something that I need to know." She pressed her hands together, closed her pretty eyes. "Like I've mentioned before, a little less than a year ago, I went through a pretty bad breakup."

"What happened?" She'd never shared the details with him, although he'd often wondered.

She shook her head, her mouth mashed down in anger. "I don't want to talk about that now. I just want you to know that my trust in my ex was broken. I can forgive him, but, I can't forget about what happened." She looked directly into his eyes again. "My whole point is, I'm leery about dating right now, and before we can move forward, I need answers to my questions."

He leaned forward, rested his elbows on his thighs, and dropped his forehead into his hands. *Lord, I really need your help here.* He needed to tell her the truth. "Remember when your family went on vacation one week during the summer?"

"Yes, I remember."

"I went to a party with some of my friends, got drunk, ended up sleeping with Salina, and got her pregnant. When she started showing—"

"She let everybody know that you were the father of her baby and I refused to believe her."

"I honestly didn't know if the baby was mine. Salina didn't have a good reputation. When my mom was offered a job in Starrick County, over two hours away, she took it. I told her about Salina. My mom's always felt guilty about my not having a father. She met Salina and liked her. She knew that Salina was going to be turned out of her foster home when she turned eighteen, and my mom was all about doing the right thing. Salina came with us when we moved, but, my mom told me that it was best if I ceased contact with you. I'd already hurt you enough and she wanted me to see if I could grow to love Salina, given time."

"What happened after that?"

"When Lisa was born we had a paternity test done and it was proven that she was mine. Being with Salina during her pregnancy, she told me about her life, we spent time together and I grew to respect her. That respect grew into love. In due time, I did learn to love Salina and contacting you just didn't seem right. Looking back now, I probably should not have followed my mom's advice and reached out to you anyway. I probably should have at least let you know what happened and why I'd made that decision."

She nodded. "Thanks for telling me, and for being honest."

"Kim, I like you, I like you a lot. I'm falling for you hard and I want you to give me a chance. I promise to always be honest with you. I rely on the Lord so much now. I've changed so much since we were teenagers."

She didn't say anything, just continued staring out the window, at the Christmas lights winking across the street. He'd give almost anything to know what she was thinking. Kim had always gotten this deep, pensive look whenever she was thinking hard about something.

"Luke, I'd like to date you, too. As you know, I've changed, and I think we need to give each other another chance."

She'd said yes! "I promise I'll do my best not to hurt you." He pulled Kim into his arms and kissed her.

CHAPTER 9

KIM GRINNED, ADMIRING THE SKATERS through the glassed wall of the Bethlehem Ice Skating Rink. Luke sat beside her, holding her hand. Shrieks and laughter floated around them as people skidded by and Lisa skated past, decently balanced on her rented ice skates.

The rink was decorated with red and green blinking Christmas lights. A giant snowman had been posted at the front of the rink. Sighing, full of content, she leaned into Luke's arms. Empty Styrofoam cups and dirty paper plates littered their table. They'd already feasted on a lunch of hot chocolate and greasy cheeseburgers. After eating, Lisa had been eager to go back onto the ice, but, Luke had made her wait for a half hour to give her food time to digest. Once he'd said it was okay for her to go back on the ice, the child had literally flown out the door and onto the ice with her skates.

She stared at Lisa as she whizzed on the ice. "It's amazing that Lisa has such good balance on her skates." Kim had fallen twice, and had not been too eager about going back onto the rink.

Snuggling in Luke's arms, she watched the skaters, enjoying their time together. "Salina took Lisa ice skating a lot. Lisa's been bugging me to bring her all month, but, I haven't had time."

Since they'd decided to start dating, Kim had enjoyed the time she'd spent with Luke over the last week. Luke came to the cookie bakery every afternoon and they had lunch together. He called her every morning before he headed out to work. When he came to pick up Lisa from the bakery, Kim would leave with them, and they spent time together every evening. She cooked dinner every night and Lisa had confided how nice it was to have home-cooked meals that were not burned to a crisp.

In spite of her father's silent protests, she got closer to Luke each day. She could tell by the way her dad scrutinized Luke, silently finding fault with him, that he didn't care for their budding relationship. As a matter of fact, she felt that her dad would have more openly objected to her relationship with Luke. However, she felt that he didn't want to rock the boat since she was now getting along with him since they'd had their talk about Tina.

Weird, she knew how strange it was, but, she really was falling in love with Luke Barnes and she didn't know what to do about it. She loved the way he cared for his daughter. She loved the way he cared about her. She loved to hear his smooth, deep voice and when he looked at her with his mesmerizing dark brown eyes, she literally swooned. She loved the way he furrowed his cute brow when he was concentrating on a Calculus problem.

She also loved the way he worshipped the Lord.

They talked about scriptures, God, and life in general. At times, she felt she could just sit and talk to Luke Barnes forever.

She thought about him all the time and she'd even burned a pan of cookies the other day, day dreaming about Luke. She'd forgotten to set her oven timer, and that's when she knew she'd fallen helplessly in love with Luke Barnes. She honestly had no idea if he felt the same way.

They'd only been seriously dating for one week, which made her deep feelings even scarier. Was it possible to fall in love in such a short period of time, or was she just infatuated? Was she confused? Should she trust her feelings, ignoring her logic?

Luke touched her face. "What are you thinking about? You look serious."

If he only knew what she'd been thinking about, she didn't know how he'd react. She smiled, forcing herself to look utterly happy. There was no way she wanted to admit that she'd been wondering if Luke was in love with her. "How did you do on your final exam?"

Grinning, Luke pulled out his cell phone. "Our grades were posted this morning." He accessed the site where the professor posted their grades and showed her the display. Kim shrieked.

"You got an A!"

He nodded, slipping his phone back into his pocket. "Since I got an A on the final exam, and I got lower grades on the mid-term and quizzes, my final grade for the class is a B." He grinned, pulling her into his arms. "I couldn't have done it without you." Kim didn't know about that. After all, Luke had studied hard for his exam. Sure, she'd tutored him, but, he'd done a lot of work studying for his test. "School is out for the winter break and Lisa doesn't have school for a couple of weeks either. I want us to have the best Christmas ever."

Luke leaned toward her, kissing her. She closed her eyes, enjoying the sweet nectar of his kiss. Their table rattled, disturbing their kiss. Kim glanced at Lisa, who'd toddled to the table on her skates. "You two are kissing! Does this mean you're going to get married?"

Luke pushed the door open to John's Sandwich Shop. Kim had mentioned that her dad often ate dinner here with his elderly friends. He spotted James Taylor, Kim's father, sitting at a table, playing checkers. The TV was turned onto CNN and the murmur of male voices filled the place. James was not expecting him, and he didn't want to make him mad by interrupting his game.

James happened to look up, spotted Luke at the door. Luke nodded at Kim's dad. James scowled, as if he were angry that Luke was invading his game time with his friends. He might as well get this over with. He approached the table. "Hi, Mr. Taylor." Luke offered his hand for a handshake, but, James ignored his outstretched hand. Kim's dad was *not* happy to see him. "Can I talk to you?"

James took a battered newspaper from the table, mumbled an apology to his checker partner. "We can finish later."

Luke found a table in the corner, away from the

rest of the small crowd. He eyed the menu which was scrawled across a chalkboard in front of the bar area. "Have you eaten?" He figured if he offered to buy her dad a sandwich, it might put him in a better mood.

"I already ate." James's gaze was steady, and he looked at Luke as if he were up to no good.

Luke scratched the back of his head, cleared his throat. Looked like this was going to be harder than he thought. But, if he stood a chance of things working out between him and Kim, then he wanted her dad to accept him. His palms became sweaty, so, he wiped them on his faded Levis. His palms always sweated when he was nervous or upset. He wiggled his toes, glanced down at his feet. He'd worn his hiking boots and his old sweat-shirt. Maybe he should've dressed better so that he looked more respectable.

"I know you didn't come over here to sit and stare at your clothes." James's gruff authoritative voice interrupted the silence at their table.

Luke cleared his throat again. He wasn't partic-ularly afraid of Kim's dad, but, he was leery about his non-acceptance of him into his daughter's life. He was falling in love with Kim, and James's frosty attitude towards him did little to allow their relationship to move forward. In spite of her dad explaining his reasons for favoring Tina, Luke still figured Kim's relationship with her dad was some-what tenuous. He figured if he bonded with James, and James accepted him, it might help solidify Luke's relationship with Kim and Kim's relation-ship with her dad. It wouldn't hurt to try. "Mr. Taylor, I wanted to thank you."

"Thank me for what? Allowing you to try to take advantage of my daughter?" He narrowed his dark eyes, his mouth set in a tense line.

That was uncalled for, but, it wouldn't help for him to get defensive against Kim's dad now. "I'm talking about Lisa." James's dark face softened and he smiled just a bit. "Lisa likes working with Kim. She's been happier since she's been in your bakery." He paused, figuring he needed to tell Mr. Taylor everything. "I think she still misses her mom."

James Taylor's frosty attitude melted as soon as he heard about Lisa's mother. "Where's her mom? Did she leave you?"

He shook his head. "No, sir. She was hit by a drunk driver. She died."

James seemed speechless. He finally seemed to find his voice as he called out to the man behind the bar, ordered two sodas and some chips and dip. After they'd been served, he finally spoke. "Sorry about your wife. Was she the girl you got pregnant back in high school?"

Luke nodded, surprised that the people in Bethlehem still remembered that. "We had a good marriage while it lasted."

"Look, I like having your kid around the bakery, but, that doesn't mean I want you kissing my daughter. You hurt her pretty bad and I haven't forgotten about that."

Luke popped open his can of soda, poured it into the glass filled with ice, gathering his thoughts. "Sorry, but that happened a long time ago and I've changed." He took a deep breath, took a sip from his soda. "I'm a parent now, and I understand why you didn't want me dating Kim in high school." Heck, if a man had treated Lisa the way he'd treated Kim, he probably wouldn't want his daughter around that man ever again. "If someone treated Lisa that way, I'd feel the same as you." He ate a few chips before he continued speaking. "I'm a Christian now, Mr. Taylor. I'm honest and when something bothers me, I go to the Lord."

"Lots of folks say they're Christian, but, that doesn't mean they're truthful."

"No, sir, it doesn't. But, I'm not accountable for people who don't do their best to be faithful to Jesus. Jesus is my number one priority, my next priority is providing for my daughter."

Since James didn't speak, Luke took that as a signal to tell James all he needed to know about his life. He told James his regrets about leaving Bethlehem without saying good-bye to Kim. He then told of Salina's untimely death.

"I'm trying to raise my daughter, provide a better life for her. I need to get my college degree to do that. Kim really helped me to pass my Calculus class." He took a deep breath. "It's hard raising Lisa without a mom. I don't know what I'm going to do when she's a teenager. Being around Kim seems to help Lisa. Spending time with Kim has made her happier." Luke finally told him about his salvation and how Jesus had been guiding him since before Salina's death. "Mr. Taylor, I was mad at God after my wife died. I didn't go to church for six months, but, I figured I shouldn't let my daughter see me be so bitter. She was suffering, too, and we found a bit of peace by going back to church, worshipping the Lord." He'd been talking for over two hours. John had brought over more sodas and chips, and

Luke's throat felt dry from talking so much. He couldn't remember the last time he'd talked for so long without stopping. Surprisingly, James had listened, not interrupting him.

The sandwich shop was closing down and Luke figured it was time to leave. When he exited the shop with James Taylor, he breathed a sigh of relief when James now shook his offered hand. "Mr. Taylor, I love your daughter. I'm not trying to take advantage of her."

"See that you treat her with respect and you won't have a problem from me," James warned.

CHAPTER 10

LUKE CLUTCHED THE PACKAGE THAT the clerk had wrapped at the store. It was three days before Christmas and with Lisa's help, he'd purchased a special gift for Kim. He hoped she liked it. He was taking her out to a fancy restaurant for dinner. He'd gotten his neighbor to babysit Lisa just so that he could go on a special Christmas date with Kim. He knocked on Kim's door and she opened it, looking classy. She wore a red, fancy dress and high-heeled shoes. She looked nice and he could imagine just standing here, looking at her forever. She shivered, so he stepped inside, gave her the wrapped package. "Merry Christmas."

She grinned, accepting his gift, placing it under the tree. "Thank you."

She removed a decorated package from underneath the tree, handed it to him. "Merry Christmas." He accepted the package, placing it back underneath the tree.

"I'll leave it here for now. I'll get it to take home with me when I drop you off after dinner."

"Sounds good." She found her coat and he held

it for her as she slipped her slim arms into the sleeves. After she'd buttoned her coat, they went out onto the porch and she locked the door. They held hands as they walked to his car and he opened her door for her. She got in and he turned on some Christmas music. The tune of Nat King Cole's *A Christmas Song* resonated in his car.

Luke swallowed, wiped his sweaty hands on his pants. As he drove toward The Italian Cottage, the fanciest restaurant in Bethlehem, Kim's lovely voice floated above the festive Christmas music. "What's going on between you and my dad?"

He resisted the urge to smile, not wanting to spoil his surprise. "What do you mean?"

She playfully shoved his arm, grinning. "You know what I mean."

Kim still didn't know about the private visit he'd recently had with her father. They'd cleared the air, and now, when he came to fetch Lisa at the bakery, instead of greeting him with a cool, wordless nod, Kim's dad met him at the door with a smile and a handshake. Her dad asked him questions about his job, and they'd even watched a football game on TV. They'd gotten pretty friendly and he'd seen Kim looking puzzled over the change in his relationship with her dad. This was the first time she'd openly asked him about it.

"Aren't you glad that I'm getting along with your father now?"

She shrugged, still looking pensive. "Yeah, but, I still think something's up. My dad doesn't warm up to people that he doesn't like too easily."

"Oh, your dad didn't like me very much?" He couldn't resist the teasing tone to his voice.

"Oh, you know what I mean. Why are you two so friendly?"

He shrugged. "Why not?"

They'd arrived at the restaurant and he parked. After they'd entered, Kim smiled, eyeing the twinkling festive Christmas lights strung around the fancy restaurant. Soft, classical Christmas music filled the air as they made their way to their table. The waiter gave them their menus and as they glanced at the selections, Luke decided he simply couldn't wait any longer. He wiped his sweaty hands on his pants before focusing on Kim. "Kim, we need to talk."

Her dark eyes appeared weary as she set her menu down. "Okay. Is everything all right?"

Everything would be perfectly fine if her answer was yes. He pressed the box into her hand. "Will you marry me?"

Her mouth dropped open and her fingers shook as she opened the velvet box, studying the diamond solitaire ring nestled within the confines of the box. When she remained silent, his heart filled with dread. Why wasn't she saying yes? "Luke, this ring is so pretty."

That's all she had to say? "Kim, I love you. I want to marry you." He paused, gathered his thoughts. "Lisa loves you, too. She wants you to be her mom."

She closed the box, hesitating. She didn't want to marry him. He could tell. Spending time with Kim, over the past month, had been some of the best days of his life. He knew he wanted to see her as soon as he woke up every morning, and he wanted her to be the last person he saw before he went to bed every night. He wanted to hold her, love her and spend his entire life with her.

But, he didn't tell her any of these things. He just couldn't. From her strange reaction, it appeared that she didn't want to hear about all of the things he loved about her. It would sound like he was begging for her to say yes if he suddenly started telling her how much he craved to see her each day. He balled his nervous hands into fists, struggled to remain calm. He'd been so sure that she'd say yes. Maybe she didn't love him after all.

"I love you, too, Luke."

This was a shocking surprise. "But, you don't want to marry me."

"I didn't say that." She closed the box, slid it over to his side of the table. "It's just that…" Her dark eyes appeared pensive and sad as she gazed at the couples dining at the other tables. The festive lights strung around the room and the Christmas music crooning from the speakers gave the room a mystic, holiday feel.

He needed to put her at ease. He took her hand, squeezed her fingers. "Honey, tell me what you're thinking about." The waiter approached their table to take their order, interrupting the tense moment. They ordered and while they feasted on pasta carbonara and herbed focaccia, he listened to Kim's smooth, pretty voice as she told of what happened to her almost one year ago.

"I fell in love with a lawyer named Bill. The accounting firm where I worked had commissioned him for a case. Through our day jobs, we crossed paths and I fell in love with him. It happened so quickly, my mind was spinning. At the time, I honestly couldn't recall feeling happier.

When he proposed, I accepted." She stopped eating, her pretty dark eyes looking dejected. "I was anxious to bring him home to Bethlehem. For once, I wanted to prove to my dad that I was capable of finding a good, educated, well-to-do man like my sister Tina. For once, I thought my dad would finally be proud of me."

"But your dad never met him, did he?" He had to wonder if Kim was really in love with Bill, or, if she was just infatuated with the idea of bringing home a man who was just as good as Tina's husband, desperate to win her father's approval.

She shook her head, put her fork down. She rubbed her forehead, as if talking about this brought her pain. "Are you all right?"

"I'm fine." She pressed her hands together before focusing on him again. "The reason why I never brought Bill home to Bethlehem is because I caught him cheating on me." She shook her head, as if the memory caused her great pain. "Luke it was awful. When I confronted him about kissing that woman, he admitted that he'd been sleeping with her. He'd said that the only reason he'd had another woman was because I'd refused to sleep with him before the wedding." She shook her head, gazing down into her plate. "Luke, I have my Christian beliefs, and I'd mistakenly thought that Bill was a Christian, too. He'd seemed willing to wait until after our wedding to have sex, but, turned out he'd been lying the entire time."

Whoa, this was a load of stuff she was revealing. He took her hand, swiped her tears away. "Why didn't you tell me the details about this before?"

She shrugged, gazed into his eyes. "I guess I was

ashamed."

"I hope you don't think I'd treat you like that."

She shook her head. "No, it's just that, I was in love with Bill and things didn't work out." She took a sip from her water glass. "Now I wonder if it's okay for me and you to marry. Luke, we've only been dating for a month."

"It's one of the best months in my entire life. Are you sure you loved Bill?"

She frowned. "What do you mean?"

"Did you really love him, or, did you just love the fact that your father would approve of him?"

Her eyes widened and she jerked back, as if she'd been slapped. "How could you say that?"

"Honey, I'm not saying that was the case, but, it's something for you to think about." He pushed the ring toward her. "Do me a favor. Think about my proposal over the next week. My neighbor will baby sit Lisa during Christmas break, so, I won't let her work in the bakery over the holidays."

She took a deep breath. "Why won't you let Lisa come to the bakery?"

"Because, I'd have to see you every day when I picked her up. I'm going to leave you alone for a week and let you think about my proposal. I want you to pray and decide if you want to risk loving me, the way a wife loves a husband."

The waiter approached. "Would the two of you like cannoli for dessert?"

Luke shook his head. "Just bring me the check."

CHAPTER 11

KIM OPENED HER EYES. BRIGHT sunlight spilled into the room and she rolled out of bed and opened the curtains. She relished the contrast between the bright sunshine against the snow covering the ground. Gracious, it sure was pretty outside. The bright sunlight sparkled against the snow, causing diamond-like glitter to sparkle in the bright sunshine. They'd gotten a rare Christmas snowstorm this year and kids were already going outside, playing in the white frigid snow.

She took her cell phone from the bedside table, looking at the date. It was December 26th, the day after Christmas. Her dad had spent Christmas with her, but, had already left early this morning on a flight to go and visit Tina and her family.

She got out of bed, yawned. She'd made plans for her best friends' annual cookie exchange and sleepover. Her friends were due to come for dinner that evening, so, she still had time to plan everything. Lord knows, she needed their company today. So many thoughts were tumbling in her head that she thought her brain would explode.

During the course of the day, while she prepared her famous chunky beef stew, homemade yeast rolls and side dishes, she talked to God. She openly prayed to Him during the day as she cleaned and prepared for her evening visitors. *Lord, I really need your help. In just four weeks, I've fallen in love with Luke, but, I don't know if I should marry him. A year ago, I was in love with Bill, and he didn't take my love seriously. Will Luke continue to love me, after we get married?*

As she prepared her vanilla cookies, she recalled every moment she'd spent with Luke, beginning from the moment he turned up in her bakery on the Tuesday after Thanksgiving. Luke loved and worried about his daughter, desperately wanting a better life for her. He loved Lisa, but, most of all, he loved God. That love had been lacking when they'd dated as wild teens and Kim realized she needed to consider that when she decided if she wanted to accept his proposal.

At seven o'clock that night, her doorbell rang and she opened her door, grinning. Miraculously, Anna, Heather and Carly had all arrived at the same time and just seeing their bright happy faces made her pause, realizing how fortunate she was to have these good friends for life. They shared a group hug, and warmth and happiness swelled within her. When she pulled away from her friends, Carly touched her shoulder, her brown hair swaying. "Hey, are you okay? You're crying."

"Girls, so much has happened since Thanksgiving. I'll tell you all about it after we eat."

They entered the house, holding overnight sacks and sleeping bags. It had been a long time since

Kim had had so many people in her parents' small home. After they'd feasted on her tasty stew and rolls, she brought out a carton of milk and Carly, Anna, and Heather each placed their box of cookies on the living room coffee table. Kim opened her box of vanilla cookies and the foursome feasted in silence on four different kinds of cookies as she got caught up on all that had been happening in her friends' lives lately.

Heather cleared her throat, gesturing toward Kim. "Well, you know all about what's been happening with us. Now it's your turn, Kim. Why were you crying when we arrived?"

"Luke Barnes has asked me to marry him." There, she'd blurted out her news.

Carly, Heather and Anna turned to stare at her. Giving her friends a few moments to digest the news, she turned on some Christmas music. The sweet, soulful sound of Nat King Cole now filled the room.

Carly pursed her mouth, fingering her short hair. "I can't believe it." She paused. "You don't seem happy. Did you accept his proposal?"

Kim shook her head. "I didn't give him an answer."

Anna and Heather frowned, each of them pulling a cookie from the tray. Anna looked toward Kim. "So when he asked you, you just sat there and didn't say anything?"

"No." As Kim selected another cookie, she told about her dinner date with Luke and about everything he'd said.

Heather leaned toward Kim. "You need to give love a chance."

Carly nodded. "This guy, Bill, who you were engaged to before? Maybe you really weren't in love with him."

Kim's mouth dropped open. "But—"

Carly shook her head. "Let me finish. Maybe Luke has a point. Besides, you'd mentioned that you had Bill's ring and you used to look at it all the time, remembering your engagement to him?"

"Yes, so what?"

Anna cleared her throat. "I think Carly's trying to say that you need to be sure that you're over Bill."

Kim scoffed. "I haven't been mooning over Bill since Luke came into my life."

Heather patted her arm. "Then you need to get rid of Bill's ring. Mail it back to him or something. No need keeping reminders of him around since you're in love with Luke."

Carly raised her hand. "Let's pray about this."

So, they joined hands and Carly's voice lifted up to the Lord asking for His guidance regarding Kim's feelings toward Luke. When the prayer was over, Kim figured out what she needed to do.

The next day, Kim knocked on Luke's door. "Who is it?" Lisa asked from behind the door.

"It's Kim."

Lisa opened the door. "Ms. Kim!" She hugged Kim, pulling her into the house with her skinny arms. "Dad said I couldn't help you make cookies for a whole week! He said you needed to think."

The girl released Kim, looked right into Kim's eyes. "Did you think enough?"

Kim laughed, pulling the package she'd been hiding behind her back. "Merry Christmas." She'd forgotten to give Kim's Christmas gift to Luke and after her cookie sleepover, had found the gift nestled under her tree. She'd bought Lisa a new outfit.

Lisa ripped off the bright red paper, grinning. "These jeans and this shirt are awesome! Thanks Ms. Kim." She hugged her again, just as Luke entered the living room. His dark eyes appeared apprehensive.

"Lisa, go up to your room."

"But, Dad—"

"Go to your room. I'll let you know when it's okay to come out."

Huffing, Lisa went into her room and closed the door. Luke took   Kim's hand and led her to the couch. They sat, and he gave her a frank look, remaining silent. Kim figured he was giving her time to say what she needed to say without rushing her. "Luke, I've been thinking about your proposal." She took a deep breath, finding joy and comfort from his holding her hand.

"Yes?"

She smiled, joy rushing through her like a geyser. "My answer is yes. Luke I want to spend the rest of my life loving you as your wife!"

Whooping, Luke pulled her into his arms, and they shared an amazing kiss. Lisa rushed into the room, grinning. "Dad, is it okay to come out of my room now?"

Laughing, the threesome hugged as Kim mentally started making plans for her wedding day.

KIM'S VANILLA COOKIES

3 3/4 cups all-purpose flour; more as needed
3/4 tsp. table salt
1 3/4 cup (3 ½ sticks) unsalted butter, softened
1 1/4 cup confectioners' sugar
1 egg
2 tsp. pure vanilla extract,
or the seeds scraped from one vanilla bean

Preheat oven to 350 degrees.

Whisk the flour, baking powder, and salt in a medium bowl.

Beat the butter and sugar on medium speed until light and fluffy, 3 to 4 minutes.

Add the egg and vanilla and continue to mix until well blended, about 1 minute. Reduce the speed to low, add the flour mixture, and mix until well blended, about 1 minute more.

Divide the dough into thirds. Wrap in plastic and chill for 4 hours. Working with one third of dough at a time, roll with a rolling pin and cut into shapes.

If rolling pin sticks to the dough, dust dough with flour or place wax paper over dough before rolling.

Bake until the edges and bottoms of the cookies are golden about 11 minutes. Repeat with each third, re-rolling the unused dough and cutting into shapes.

Frost and decorate as desired.

ABOUT CECELIA

I spent the first ten years of my life on a military base in Aberdeen Maryland since my dad was in the Army. We moved to North East Maryland when I was about ten. I always remember the joy of opening a book, and reading mesmerizing stories that entertained me for hours! I went to the University of Maryland in College Park, earning my degree in Finance! My freshman English teacher claimed I was a great writer, and recommended that I change my major from Finance to English, but I didn't heed his wise advice!

Instead of pursuing a literary career, I worked as an accountant for a travel agency for ten years. During that time, I traveled all over the world, including the following places: Germany, France, England, Tahiti, New Zealand, Mexico, Jamaica, Bahamas, Cayman Islands, and Santo Domingo.

In 1994, I began writing for fun, and I kept doing it until I sold my first inspirational romance novel. Before I sold my novel, I wrote sweet romantic short stories regularly for national women's magazines. I've published thirty-seven of these stories. I'm now working on other novels, and you can check the books section of this website to see a list of past and future releases!

I love both secular and Christian fiction. I also love young adult fiction, and I hope to have my own young adult inspirational series someday!

I've been happily married for several years. I currently reside with my husband and son in Maryland.

CONTACT CECELIA

Website: www. ceceliadowdy.com
FaceBook: www.facebook.com/cecelia.dowdy
Twitter: www.twitter.com/cdnovelist

Email: dowdywriter@aol.com

Snail mail:

Cecelia Dowdy
P.O. Box 951
Greenbelt, MD 20768-0951

Made in the USA
Columbia, SC
07 May 2020

93607177R00055